Max
at Night

by Ed Vere

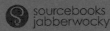
sourcebooks
jabberwocky

This is Max.

It's way past Max's bedtime.

Max is **very** sleepy.

Max has drunk his milk.

Max has brushed his teeth.

Max has cleaned behind his ears.

Now Max is going to say good night…

"Good night, Fish,"
says Max.

"Good night, Box,"
says Max.

"Good night, Spider," says Max.

"Good night, Moon,"
says Max.

But the moon is
nowhere to be seen.

"Moon...
Moon!
Where are you, Moon?"
says Max.

"Maybe I'll see Moon from outside…"

Max steps out into the starlit night.

"Good night, Night," says Max.
"Have you seen Moon?"

But the night is dark and quiet.

"Maybe I'll see Moon if I get
        a little higher," thinks Max.

Max tiptoes carefully up onto the sleeping dog.

"Good night, Dog," whispers Max.
"Have you seen Moon?"

But the sleeping dog is sleeping.

"Maybe I'll see Moon if I get
a little higher," thinks Max.

Max climbs up a tall, tall tree
and creeps out along a branch.

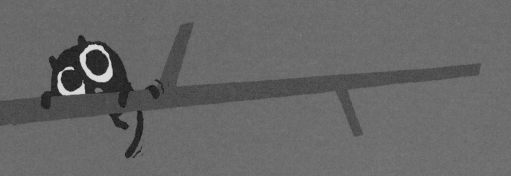

"Good night, Tree," says Max. "Do you
know where I can find Moon?"

But the tall, tall tree only rustles in the breeze.

Max climbs even higher, up among the rooftops.

"Good night, Rooftops," says Max.
"Have **you** seen Moon?"

But the rooftops are silent.

"Hmm, maybe if I get much higher…"
thinks Max. "Maybe from the tallest building?"

Max climbs up

and up

and up.

"Good night, Tallest Building," says Max.

"Can you see Moon?"

But the tallest building says nothing.

"Oh, Moon.

Where **are** you, Moon?"

says Max.

Max is very tired, but he climbs up
even higher,
to the **highest** of the high hills,
where the wind blows cold and strong.

"Good night, Hill," says Max.
"Please tell me, have you seen Moon?"

But the highest of the high hills
just whistles in the wind.

Max has had enough…

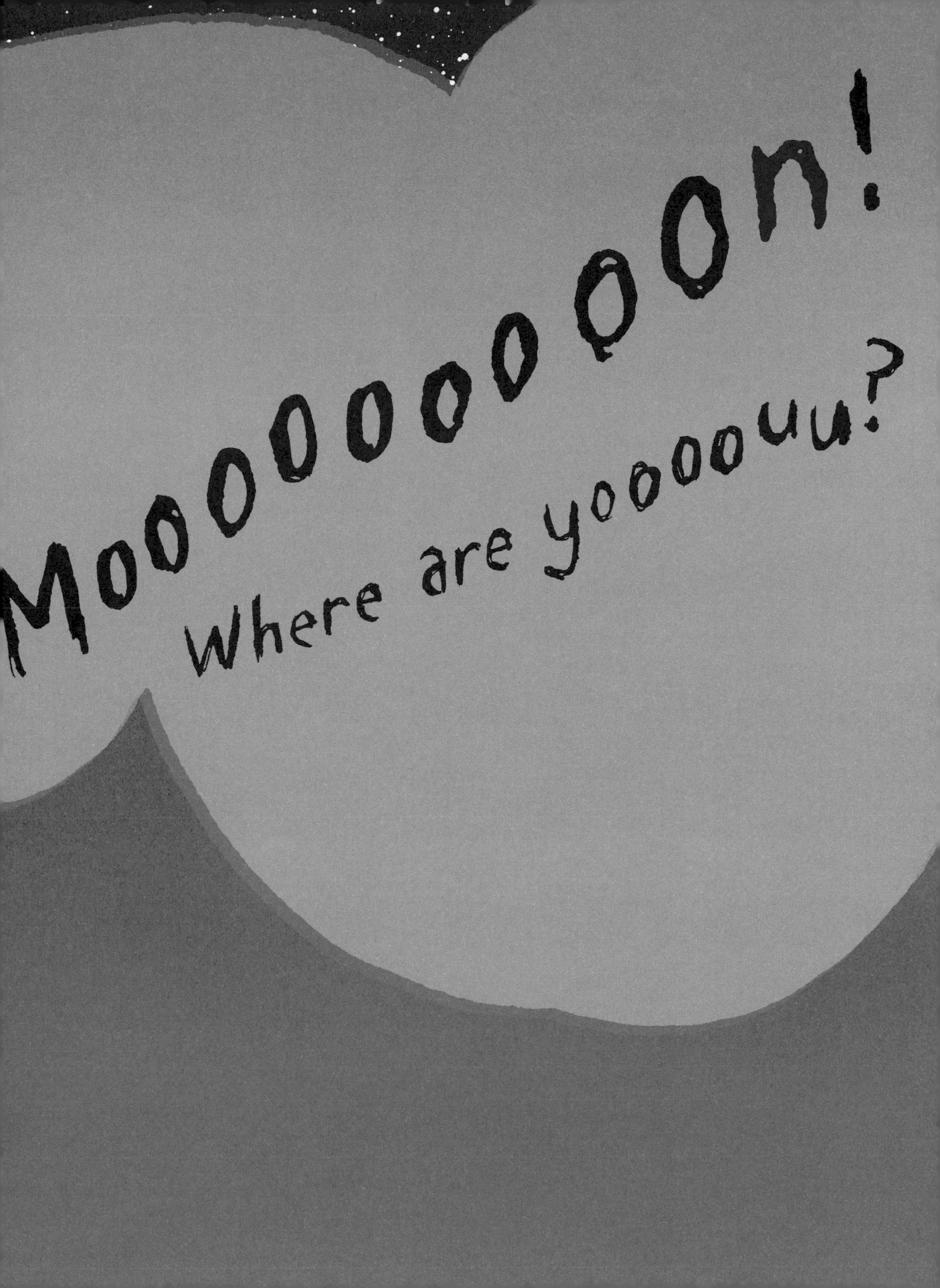
Mooooooooon!
Where are yoooouu?

Up on the highest of the high hills,
the wind hears Max and blows
and blows
and blows
the clouds away…

And there, full and brilliant
in the night sky...

"Moon!"

"Good night, Max," whispers Moon.
"And thank you very much for coming."

"Good night, Moon," yawns Max.
"It's been a long, long night.
Now I can go to bed."

"Max," calls Moon across the night sky.
"Did you know that I **can** hear you
when you say good night at home?"

"Oh," says Max. "Now you tell me!
Well, **thank you**,
that's very good to know."

Max is tired and happy.

He walks back along the rooftops…

and clambers down
the tall, tall tree.

Max creeps carefully over the sleeping dog,

and sleepy, very sleepy—
he climbs the stairs to bed.

"Sleep tight, Max," says Moon.

But Max doesn't hear.
Max is snoring,
      snoring,
            snoring, fast asleep.

for
Anouk

Copyright © 2015 by Ed Vere
Cover images/illustrations © Ed Vere

Sourcebooks and the colophon are registered trademarks of Sourcebooks, Inc.
All rights reserved. No part of this book may be reproduced in any form or by any electronic or mechanical means including information
storage and retrieval systems—except in the case of brief quotations embodied in critical articles or reviews—without permission in
writing from its publisher, Sourcebooks, Inc.

The digitally-created illustrations incorporate pen and ink sketches and mixed media.

Published by Sourcebooks Jabberwocky, an imprint of Sourcebooks, Inc.
P.O. Box 4410, Naperville, Illinois 60567-4410
(630) 961-3900
Fax: (630) 961-2168
www.sourcebooks.com
Originally published in 2015 in the United Kingdom by Puffin Books, an imprint of Penguin Random House.
Library of Congress Cataloging-in-Publication data in on file with the publisher.
Source of Production: RR Donnelley Asia Printing Solutions Limited, Kwun Tong, Kowloon, Hong Kong
Date of Production: May 2016
Printed and bound in China.
10 9 8 7 6 5 4 3 2 1

edvere.com
@edvere